Collins English Library
Series editors: K R Cripwell and Lewis Jones

A library of graded readers for students of English as a foreign lan~
for reluctant native readers. The books are graded in six l~
Structure, vocabulary, idiom and sentence len~
to principles laid down in detail in *A T~*
Library. The books are listed b~
vocabulary of 300 words and ap~
words, 4: 1500 words, 5: 2000 w~
are asterisked are accompanied b~

Level One

Inspector Ho~
Inspector Hol~
Crocodile! *K R*
Four Short Stor~
Fast Money *K R*
It's a Trick! *Lewi~*
The Story of Macbeth *from Shakespeare*
Tin Lizzie* *Jane Homeshaw*
Dead in the Morning* *Jane Homeshaw*
Letters from the Dead* *Jane Homeshaw*
Taxi! *Jane Homeshaw*
The Pathfinders* *Jane Homeshaw*
Inspector Holt: Cats in the Dark* *John Tully*
Inspector Holt and the Chinese Necklace *John Tully*
Journey to Universe City *Leslie Dunkling*
Three Folk Tales* *Margaret Naudi*
The Man with Three Fingers *John Tully*
Fastline UK *Jane Homeshaw*
The Grey Rider *Steve Rabley*
Love Me Tomorrow *Jane Homeshaw*

Level Two

The Magic Garden *K R Cripwell*
Muhammad Ali: King of the Ring *John Tully*
Inspector Holt Gets His Man* *John Tully*
The Canterville Ghost* *Oscar Wilde*
The Prince and the Poor Boy *Mark Twain*
Inspector Holt: The Bridge* *John Tully*
Oliver Twist *Charles Dickens*
Two Roman Stories *from Shakespeare*
The Titanic is Sinking* *K R Cripwell*
The Wrestler *K R Cripwell*
Madame Tussaud's* *Lewis Jones*
Three Sherlock Holmes Adventures* *A Conan Doyle*
The Story of Scotland Yard *Lewis Jones*
The Charlie Chaplin Story* *Jane Homeshaw*
Charles and Diana *Margery Morris*
A King's Love Story *K R Cripwell*
Dangerous Earth *Jane Homeshaw*
Chariots of Fire* *W J Weatherby*
Shark Attack *Jan Keane*
The Complete Robot: Selected Stories *Isaac Asimov*
Roadie *Chris Banks*
The Mystery of Dr Fu Manchu *Sax Rohmer*

Level Three

Climb a Lonely Hill *Lilith Norman*
Custer's Gold *Kenneth Ulyatt*
Gunshot Grand Prix *Douglas Rutherford*
David Copperfield* *Charles Dickens*
Born Free *Joy Adamson*

Five Ghost Stories* *Viola Huggins*
Three English Kings *from Shakespeare*
An American Tragedy *Theodore Dreiser*
Six American Stories* *N Wymer*
Emma and I *Sheila Hocken*
Little Women *Louisa M Alcott*
The Picture of Dorian Gray* *Oscar Wilde*
Maimunah *David Hill*
Marilyn Monroe *Peter Dainty*
Bruce Springsteen *Toni Murphy*
Is That It? *Bob Geldof*
Short Stories *Oscar Wilde*
A Room with a View *E M Forster*
The Importance of Being Ernest *Oscar Wilde*
The Lost World *Sir Arthur Conan Doyle*
Arab Folk Tales *Helen Thomson*
Computers: From Beads to Bytes *Peter Dewar*

Level Four

The White South *Hammond Innes*
A Christmas Carol *Charles Dickens*
King Solomon's Mines* *H Rider Haggard*
Jane Eyre *Charlotte Brontë*
Pride and Prejudice *Jane Austen*
Dr Jekyll and Mr Hyde* *R L Stevenson*
Huckleberry Finn *Mark Twain*
Landslide *Desmond Bagley*
Nothing is the Number When You Die *Joan Fleming*
The African Child *Camara Laye*
The Lovely Lady and other Stories *D H Lawrence*
Airport International *Brian Moynahan*
The Secret Sharer and other Sea Stories *Joseph Conrad*
Death in Vienna? *K E Rowlands*
Hostage Tower* *Alistair MacLean*
The Potter's Wheel *Chukwuemeka Ike*
Tina Turner *Stephen Rabley*
Campbell's Kingdom *Hammond Innes*

Level Five

The Guns of Navarone *Alistair MacLean*
Geordie *David Walker*
Wuthering Heights *Emily Brontë*
Where Eagles Dare *Alistair MacLean*
Wreck of the Mary Deare *Hammond Innes*
I Know My Love *Catherine Gaskin*
Among the Elephants *Iain and Oria Douglas-Hamilton*
The Mayor of Casterbridge *Thomas Hardy*
Sense and Sensibility *Jane Austen*
The Eagle has Landed *Jack Higgins*
Middlemarch *George Eliot*
Victory *Joseph Conrad*
Experiences of Terror* *Roland John*
Japan: Islands in the Mist *Peter Milward*

Level Six

Doctor Zhivago *Boris Pasternak*
The Glory Boys *Gerald Seymour*
In the Shadow of Man *Jane Goodall*
Harry's Game *Gerald Seymour*
House of a Thousand Lanterns *Victoria Holt*
Hard Times *Charles Dickens*
Sons and Lovers *D H Lawrence*
The Dark Frontier *Eric Ambler*
Vanity Fair *William Thackeray*
Inspector Ghote Breaks an Egg *H R F Keating*

Collins English Library Level 4

HAMMOND INNES
CAMPBELL'S KINGDOM

Abridged and simplified by Viola Huggins

COLLINS
E·L·T

Original edition © Hammond Innes 1952
This edition © Collins 1988

Published in Great Britain by
William Collins Sons and Co Ltd
Glasgow G4 0NB
Printed in Great Britain by Martins of Berwick

First published in Collins English Library, 1988
Reprinted: 1989

ISBN 0 00 370175 1

Stills from the film "Campbell's Kingdom" by courtesy of
the Rank Organisation plc.
Stills supplied by the National Film Archive, London.
Map illustration by Francis Scholes.
Cover photo by permission of Barnaby's Picture Library.
Cover design by Daniel Lim.

Chapter One

My name is Bruce Wetheral. My story begins in London. The year was 1950, not many years after the war. My doctor had just given me some bad news.

"I'm sorry, Mr. Wetheral," he said. "I have your X-ray here. You're very ill, and I'm afraid we can do nothing to help you. You have a serious disease of the blood."

I looked at him. "Am I going to die?" I asked.

"Yes."

"When?"

"You have perhaps six months. Not more."

I went home to my empty flat. I wasn't married. I was thirty-six. I felt afraid, alone, and very ill.

I worked in an office, but I didn't like it much. I had fought in the war, of course. I was a good soldier, they said.

"What am I going to do?" I thought.

There was a man, a stranger, outside my front door.

"Are you waiting for me?" I asked.

"Are you Mr Bruce Wetheral?" the man said.

"Yes," I replied.

"My name is Fothergill. I'm a lawyer," said the stranger. "I have some news for you." He smiled at me. "Can I talk to you?"

"Come in," I said.

We went inside and sat down. I felt very tired.

"First I must ask you some questions," said Fothergill. "Your name is Bruce Campbell Wetheral?"

"Yes."

"Your mother's father was Stuart Campbell, who came from Scotland?"

"Yes," I replied coldly. I didn't want to talk about my grandfather.

"Did you know him?"

"I met him once. He was in prison in this country. When he came out of prison, I was with my mother. We didn't see him again."

"Why was Stuart Campbell in prison?"

"He was a thief," I replied. "He said there was oil in the Rocky Mountains in Canada. People gave him money to find it. There was no oil. A business friend, Paul Morton, took all the money and left the country. They never found him."

"Mr Wetheral," said the lawyer. "Your grandfather is dead. He had some land, a high valley in the Rockies. He lived there alone. People called it Campbell's Kingdom. It belongs to you now."

He gave me a paper. It stated my grandfather's last wishes. There was a letter with it.

"So my grandfather went back to Canada after he came out of prison." I said. "I can't believe it.

6

Why?"

"He said he knew there was oil in his Kingdom. He wanted to find it, and pay the people who lost their money. He had some friends left. Last summer, one of them gave him money to search for oil again. But there was no oil, Mr. Wetheral."

He took a paper from his bag. "In Canada a man called Peter Trevedian wants to buy the land. He wants to build a dam across the end of the valley. This dam will flood the valley with water to make electricity. You'll get about ten thousand dollars."

I thought for a minute. "I don't want ten thousand dollars," I said. "I want to see the Kingdom before I sell it."

"Mr. Wetheral, it's ten thousand kilometres away in the Canadian Rocky Mountains. Take the money. Sign this paper."

"No," I said. "I'll phone you, Mr. Fothergill. Now I want to think. Good afternoon."

When Fothergill had gone I opened the letter from my grandfather. It began, "*For my grandson.*" He asked me in his letter for my help. He wanted me to prove that he was not a thief. He was sure there was oil in his Kingdom. He had formed a company to develop it, and now he had left this company to me. In his house in the Kingdom I would find more details of his search for oil.

I read the letter again, and in my mind I now had a picture of my grandfather. I could see him sitting alone in his home in the high mountains of Canada. His honesty shone through like a clean wind out of the high mountains. I was ashamed because I had believed he was a thief.

I promised myself to do what my grandfather asked. And now I felt stronger, no longer alone and no longer afraid. I had something important to do, and time was short.

I read the papers again, and looked at a newspaper report of my grandfather's death. The report was in the *Calgary Daily*, and spoke warmly of Stuart Campbell.

I put the newspaper down. I went over to the table, and picked up the sale paper. If I signed it, the lawyer said, I might get ten thousand dollars in six months' time. But the doctor said I had only six months to live.

I decided to leave my dull work in London and go to Canada. I would carry out my grandfather's last wishes. I tore the sale paper into pieces.

Chapter Two

It took me a week to get to Calgary in Alberta, Canada, by plane and train. While on the train I received a telegram from a Canadian lawyer, Mr. Acheson. He asked me to come to his office in Calgary immediately. I felt tired but my mind was racing as I sat back in the train carriage, enjoying my first view of Canada.

In Calgary I went to Acheson's office. As I went in, I noticed a door opposite. The name of the company caught my eye. It was the Roger Fergus Oil Development Company. Next door to it was the office of Louis Winnick, Oil Engineer. Another door had the name Henry Fergus, The Larsen Mining and Development Company.

Acheson said, "You told Fothergill you don't want to sell."

"No," I said, "not until I've seen the place."

"You're wasting your time," said Acheson. "Roger Fergus looked for oil in Campbell's Kingdom last summer. A report from Louis Winnick proves that there is no oil. The land is worth very little. And the rights belong to Mr. Roger Fergus, so you can't drill for oil.'

"I'd still like to see the place," I said.

"It'll be difficult at this time of the year. Here, take this report and read it. Come and see me again at about five."

On the way out I looked at the door opposite, with the words the Roger Fergus Oil Development Company. I opened the door and went in. A girl told me Mr. Fergus was ill at home.

"He was a friend of my grandfather," I said. She telephoned Roger Fergus at home. I could go and see him, she said.

At his home I was received by a nurse.

"Five minutes, that's all," she said, as she took me into the room.

I saw a man seated in a wheel chair. He was a

big man, with broad shoulders and a mass of white hair. He had a fine face, but he was clearly ill and in pain.

"So you're Stuart's grandson," he said. "Sit down. He often spoke of you. He hoped that one day you'd be managing an oilfield for him. The old fool!" His voice was surprisingly gentle.

"What brought you out to Canada?" he asked.

I told him the whole story then, including the doctor's report on my health.

"Well, if you want to throw good money after bad and drill a well, do it."

"I can't," I said laughing. "You're the only person who could do that. You own the rights. You're the only one who can drill there."

"Yes, I'd forgotten that," he said. He leaned back with closed eyes. "I wonder... why was Boy Bladen so interested? He was like Stuart. He did the tests, and he gave the figures to Winnick. Winnick is an honest man. And his report says no oil."

The nurse came in, and I stood up. Fergus held out his hand to me.

"Good luck," he said. "I'm glad you came. If the doctor is right, we'll perhaps meet again soon. We'll have plenty of time to talk then."

Chapter Three

I returned to my hotel. At the desk in the entrance a man was paying his hotel bill. He said to the clerk, "If a man called Jack Harbin asks for me, tell him I've gone back to Jasper."

"OK, Jeff," replied the clerk. "I'll tell him."

Jasper was a town near the Yellowhead Pass, the gateway into the Rocky Mountains. And Campbell's kingdom was about eighty kilometres from Jasper.

I asked Jeff if he could take me with him in his car.

Jeff Hart was a friendly fellow.

"OK, hurry up," he said. "I've got to be in Edmonton by tea time."

I didn't have time to think about Acheson until I was in Jeff's car, and then I didn't care. I was moving one step nearer to the Kingdom.

About four o'clock the following day we were on the road to Jasper. Then I got my first sight of the Rocky Mountains. They rose up, a solid wall of snow and ice and cold grey rock.

"Do you know a man called Johnnie Carstairs?" I asked Jeff. According to the *Calgary Daily*, Johnnie was the man who found my grandfather's body, and the newspaper report said he came from Jasper.

"Yes, I know Johnnie. He owns horses, and he acts as a guide to visitors in the summer."

We arrived at Jasper, and booked in at a hotel. By that time I was feeling tired and ill. Jeff wanted to fetch a doctor, but I stopped him. We went down to the hotel bar. Jeff contacted Johnnie Carstairs and asked him to meet us there.

"There's Johnnie now," said Jeff. I saw a big man in a sheepskin jacket. He had a kind face, brown from wind and sun. His eyes had a faraway look, as if he was always looking for a distant mountain top.

"I understand you've been asking for me, Bruce," he said smiling. I told him I was Stuart Campbell's grandson. I asked him how he had found my grandfather's body.

"Strange thing, that," said Johnnie, putting down his beer glass. "Old King Campbell was fine when we got up there. And when we came back from a week's climbing, he was lying dead, face down on the floor just inside the door."

"What do you think caused his death?"

"Old age, I think. Or perhaps he died of cold up there."

"How do I get there?" I asked.

"You won't get up there yet, not till the snow melts. That'll be in about a month."

"I can't wait that long," I said.

"Well," said Johnnie, "Max Trevedian might take you up. He acts as a guide round the little town of Come Lucky, and he drives a lorry with supplies for the town. But he's not a very pleasant man."

I told Jeff and Johnnie why I couldn't wait. I had only a few months to live.

Next day when I left they both came with me to the station. As the train left, Johnnie called to me, "Any time you need help, Bruce, there's a couple of friends here in Jasper. They'll help you. And we'll be up to see you some time," he added.

Chapter Four

The train took me part of the way. Then I found a farmer who drove me further in his lorry. At a place called Keithley Creek I was told that Max Trevedian was there. He was loading groceries into a heavy lorry.

He agreed to take me with him, and we left town just after two. The noise of the chains on the wheels of the lorry was deadened by the soft snow. We could hardly see.

I looked at my companion. He was a great ox of a man, wearing a huge coat and a cap with ear covers. His face was dark brown. He had thick lips and a broad flat nose.

"Is there a hotel in Come Lucky?" I asked. He bent his head, but didn't speak. I didn't try to talk again for some time. We travelled on through the snow, climbing continuously. I tried again.

"Do you know Campbell's Kingdom?" I asked.

He was immediately interested.

"Why do you want to go there?" he asked. "There was an old fellow who lived up there, but he's dead now. He thought there was oil there. The old fool!" His voice rose to a high angry note.

I didn't speak to him again. As it grew dark we came to the shores of a narrow lake. The small town of Come Lucky was at the head of it.

The town was half buried in snow. The wooden houses were gathered together by the side of the lake. The road continued along the shore of the lake into a valley. But we stopped outside a long wooden building. There was a notice on one of the doors: 'office of the Trevedian Company'.

Max Trevedian got out and started to unload the lorry. A man came out to help him.

"Is this the hotel?" I asked.

"No, it's for the men working on the road. Go to Mr. Mac's hotel. It's over there."

Come Lucky was once a rich town because there were gold mines near. But a fall of rock had closed them many years ago. I walked through the snow into the town. It seemed empty and dead, like a ghost town.

Mr Mac's hotel was the largest building. But it, too, had seen better days. I took a room there, and had a meal with the family in the kitchen.

Mr Mac (short for McClellan) ate with me,

and also his son James McClellan, and his wife Pauline and their children.

When they heard that I was Campbell's grandson Mr Mac and his son were not pleased. And my refusal to sell the Kingdom seemed to alarm them. James McClellan got up and went out to see Peter Trevedian, his boss.

Mr Mac said to me afterwards, "This is not your sort of country. There's no oil in the Kingdom. Bladen's report proved that. You ought to sell and go home to England. Visitors are all right in the summer. But we don't like strangers here."

I knew he was warning me.

Chapter Five

Next day I went out to have a look at Come Lucky. The snow had stopped. I walked down as far as the office of the Trevedian Company. A big lorry was outside, and the driver came out just as I reached it. He was taking some machinery up to Thunder Creek, he said. I went with him.

The lorry climbed up higher and higher among the dark woods. He showed me two great mountain tops.

"They're called Solomon's Judgment," he said, "and Campbell's Kingdom lies up there in the mountains."

My heart sank. "How far does this road go?" I asked.

"Well, it doesn't go up to the Kingdom," he laughed. "There's another six hundred metres of rock to climb."

We came round a bend in the road, and there in front of us we saw a group of men working. The road had been recently closed by a fall of rock, and they were working to clear it.

The driver got out and started to unload the machinery. I stood looking up at the two mountain tops. I could see a shelf of rock between them, like a wall.

"Here, take these glasses," said the driver "If

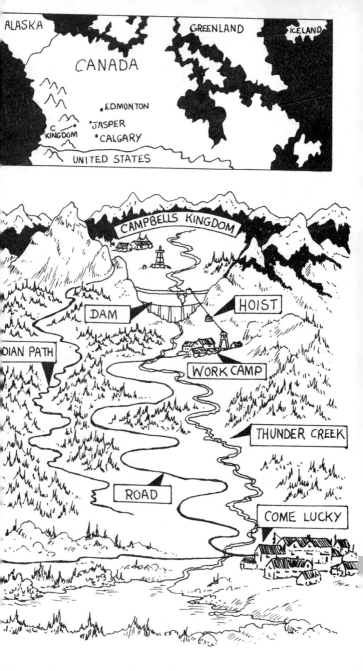

you look through these you'll get a better view."

Through the glasses I could see that the shelf between the mountains was not a shelf of rock. It was man made, not natural. It was a dam, built to hold water back. I looked again and saw that it was not complete. The centre part was missing.

"When was the dam built?" I asked the driver.

"Oh, before the war," he replied, "but they stopped work on it. They're going to complete it now and fill it in. That's what this road is for. You can see the hoist they'll use to raise the materials."

I looked again and in the distance I could just see the platform of the hoist, and the thick wires holding it.

I went to speak to the man in charge of the workmen. "Who ordered you to build this road?" I asked. "This road is being built to bring material up to finish the dam, isn't it? And if the dam is on my land..."

"It isn't on your land. The land this side of the dam belongs to Peter Trevedian, and what happens down here is nothing to do with you."

The driver shouted that he was leaving. I climbed into the lorry with him and returned to Come Lucky. Trevedian's office was locked and I went on to the hotel. While I sat there, trying to think what to do, a man came into the bar.

He was short and dark, with black hair and a coppery skin, and he had a lively manner.

"Hello, Mac," he said, coming forward into the bar, with a pleasant smile on his face.

Mr. Mac got to his feet and shook his hand.

"It's great to see you, Boy. Jean was saying the other day it was time. I've got a room for you."

"I'm going to see Jean now," said Boy. "I'll get a meal at her place."

When he had gone, Mr. Mac said, "That was Boy Bladen, the fellow who searched for oil in the Kingdom last summer. But there wasn't any."

I then remembered the words of old Roger Fergus. "Why was Boy so interested? He was like Stuart." I could hear his words now. Perhaps I could find out the truth from Boy Bladen.

Mr. Mac went on, "Bladen took his machinery up in lorries to Campbell's Kingdom. He left it there all the winter. Then the rock fell, and closed the road. He hasn't been able to get his machinery back yet."

I went out to see Peter Trevedian. As I got near to his office Boy Bladen came out quickly, and he seemed very angry about something.

Inside the office I found Trevedian. He was a man of about forty-five, strong and broad, with greying hair. His small black eyes were fastened on my face while he offered me a cigarette. He knew who I was, and he said, "Your refusal to sell the Kingdom has made great difficulties for me. The Solomon's Judgment dam has to be finished this summer. I'm being paid to get on with it. I have to clear the road and take the materials up in the hoist."

"I haven't decided to sell," I said.

He told me that a lot of people put all their money into my grandfather's company. They lost it all. My grandfather went to England to look for more money. But his business friend Paul Morton disappeared with the money, and my grandfather went to prison.

"The old timers who still live here are poor because of your grandfather," he said. "If you sell the Kingdom, then Henry Fergus will go on with his electricity plan, and Come Lucky will become a rich town again. You'll bring it back to life. What are you going to do?"

"I'll think it over," I said, and left him.

Chapter Six

I went back to the hotel, where I found Boy Bladen. I took him on one side and asked him about his work on Campbell's Kingdom. He said he checked the rock, and sent his figures to Louis Winnick in Calgary. Winnick wrote the actual report.

"Do you agree with the report?" I asked.

He didn't seem to want to answer. But at last he said, "Yes."

When he had gone I went into the kitchen where James McClellan's wife Pauline was busy working.

"Could you tell me whether there's a girl called Jean living here now?" I asked.

"Oh yes, she lives with Miss Garret and her sister," replied Pauline. "If you like, I'll take you to their house when I've put my little girl to bed."

Later Pauline led me through the unlit streets. "It's quite dangerous at night. There's no money to repair the buildings," she said.

"Tell me," I said, "is Max Trevedian the brother of Peter Trevedian, the manager of the business?"

"Yes, Max and Peter are half-brothers, I think. They're very different. Max is so big and ugly and stupid – they say he's half-mad. And Peter is the opposite."

We reached the Garrets' house and knocked. A door opened, and the yellow lamplight flooded the small entrance hall.

"Come in," said Miss Ruth Garret. She was a tiny little woman, dressed in a black dress in the fashion of my grandmother. And she knew all about me.

Her sister Sarah also welcomed me. She was very like her sister, but her face was softer. She went to fetch Jean.

I looked round the room. It was furnished just like the rooms our grandparents lived in. The whole place, including the two old ladies, with their careful way of speaking, was an old fashioned little island. It was a piece of old England in the Canadian Rockies.

"You don't look very well, Mr Wetheral," said Ruth Garret. "Have you been ill?"

"I'm getting better. I'm surprised that my grandfather agreed to the building of the dam," I said.

"Oh, it wasn't your grandfather," she said. "It was Peter Trevedian. It's on his land, you know. His father, Luke, wouldn't have done it. It meant making a lake out of Mr. Campbell's Kingdom. I'm afraid Peter is a much harder man than his father."

Jean Lucas came into the room. She was a good looking young woman with intelligent grey eyes and she was well dressed.

"I thought you would come," she said, holding out her hand. "I know what you did in the war. I didn't think you would disappoint your grandfather."

I noticed that the left side of her face was badly marked by an old wound. She took me to her own room, where a fire was burning and there were bookshelves on the walls. A big dog lay by the fire.

"I have something to give you," she said.

Chapter Seven

Jean said, "After your mother died, Stuart Campbell heard no more from England. It was only when I came here..." She looked away into the fire.

"I wrote to friends in England, and they wrote to the War Office, I think. They reported that you were a Captain in the army during the war.

You were wounded and they couldn't discover what happened to you afterwards. Why didn't you write to your grandfather?"

"I didn't know his address," I said.

"He was sent to prison. He was wrongly punished. You meant a lot to him. You were his only relation. I have some things for you."

She gave me a box. I opened it. Inside there were photographs and papers from the First World War. There were several other personal things and letters.

"I brought them here from his house," she said. "I knew what he wanted you to have. I felt sure you would come here."

"You went up to Campbell's Kingdom after his death?" I asked.

"The hoist wasn't working then. But there's an old Indian path. You can go on horseback."

I found a letter in the box addressed to myself. I began to read it.

> 'Dear Bruce,
> When you read this, the Kingdom will be yours. I shall not last the winter. And I have no longer the strength or the determination to fight for my beliefs. Today I received the report from Winnick on Bladen's work...'

I stopped reading and looked at Jean.

"I thought he died without knowing the results," I said.

"Yes, I was very glad," she said.

"But he *did* know the results," I said. And I read the letter to her.

She turned to me angrily. "How could they be

so cruel?" she said.

"There were people down in the valley who wanted to hurt him," I said. "They climbed up through a snow storm to give him the bad news before the winter closed in on him. I'd like to get my hands on the man who took that report up to him."

I read the rest of the letter. My grandfather told me he was sure there was oil. His last wish was for me to drill into the rock before they completed the dam and the water covered the Kingdom for ever.

"How am I going to get the money to do this?" I thought.

"I'll see what Bladen has to say," I said to Jean.

"Yes. He's coming to see me soon. I want you to like him. He's a strange man, but he's one of the best."

24

Later at the hotel Boy Bladen came to see me. He told me he had been talking to Jean.

"Trevedian can refuse to bring down my machinery in the hoist," he said. "But I must tell you that Winnick's report is nonsense. I sent him the figures I got from my examination of the ground in the Kingdom."

"How did you send them?"

"I sent them down by the hoist. Max Trevedian was bringing supplies up to us. I sent them down each week. They were to be sent on to Winnick. Winnick is an honest man..." He stopped. "They must have put some other figures in place of mine. Figures from unsuccessful searches."

He jumped up and started walking up and down. "I'm not surprised Peter Trevedian tries to keep my mouth shut. Jean says you want to prove that old Stuart was right. She says you have the courage to do it. But you need someone to work with you."

"She's right about the first part," I said. "But I've got no money to drill an oil well."

"If I can find the money and the machinery, will you divide the profits with me?" asked Bladen. I agreed.

"I'll go and see old Roger Fergus in Calgary. He might provide the money."

"And he owns the mining rights," I said.

"While I'm away, go up to the Kingdom by the hoist," said Bladen. "Look in the lorry I left there, and you'll find the figures I wrote down for Winnick. Mail them to Winnick. I'll leave you

25

now. You look tired. It's the height of this place. You'll soon find it easier. Goodnight."

Chapter Eight

The road was now clear. The fallen rock had been moved away. The workers were now able to drive on to the hoist. A work camp had been made there for the men, the machinery and the materials.

While waiting for a report from Boy Bladen, I went for walks with Jean. She didn't talk much, and she said nothing about herself. Then I had a telegram from Boy Bladen. He told me that old Roger Fergus had died. Bladen was sure the figures used in Winnick's report were not his. He reminded me to try and get his own figures. He had left them in a lorry in the Kingdom. He asked me to send them to Winnick.

The death of old Roger Fergus made me sad. He was ill, but I had not thought the end would come so soon. And now, I thought, the mining rights in the Kingdom would pass to his son Henry Fergus, of the Larsen Mining and Development Company. And Peter Trevedian was working for them.

Next day I went to Peter Trevedian's office. Both Peter and his half-brother Max were there. Max was loading up the lorry.

"You're going to Campbell's Kingdom today, aren't you?" said Max to his brother with a foolish look on his face.

"We're going to the dam," replied Peter. There was another workman in the lorry.

"It's the same thing. We can go together, can't we?" said Max.

"No."

"But you told me old Stuart Campbell doesn't rest. Perhaps he's still alive..."

"Shut up!" said Peter Trevedian violently. "Finish loading the lorry."

The poor fool did as he was ordered. Then Peter Trevedian turned to me. "You're not coming up in one of my lorries," he said.

I went back to the hotel. How could I get up to Campbell's Kingdom? Mr Mac said two friends were coming to see me.

"Two friends? Who were they?"

"Johnnie Carstairs and a fellow called Jeff Hart. They said they'd be here this afternoon," replied Mr. Mac.

I looked out of the window, thinking about the problems. I saw a figure on horseback riding by. It was Max Trevedian. He was a fine rider. I asked Mr. Mac, "Why does Max Trevedian want to go up to the Kingdom?"

"Oh, the man's simple. You don't need to worry about him. He's been mad for a long time. All he understands is horses."

About tea time Johnnie Carstairs and Jeff Hart arrived. They had promised to help me when I left them in Jasper. Now I was glad of their help. Jeff had met Boy Bladen, and heard about the false report. I told them all that had happened.

"Your grandfather was a fine man," said Johnnie. "I saw him in the Kingdom, and I knew him well. But luck was against him."

Later Peter Trevedian came into the bar. Johnnie went straight to the attack.

"I came here because of what I heard from Bladen," said Johnnie angrily. "You killed Stuart Campbell, an old friend of mine."

"Stop talking nonsense," said Trevedian. "I didn't touch the old man, and you know it."

"Were you afraid old Campbell would tell the newspapers that he knew about the dam?" said Johnnie.

"What do you mean?"

"You supplied bad quality material for the dam," said Johnnie. "It had been lying on the rocks by the sea after a shipwreck. A shipowner told me about it. You supplied it about 1940, when the dam was started."

Peter Trevedian nearly hit Johnnie. Then he laughed. "So I'm supposed to have killed Campbell because he knew something about the materials I supplied. What rubbish!" And Trevedian left the bar.

Johnnie said to me, "I'm going to see your friend Jean."

When he had left I asked Jeff, "What did he mean about the material for the dam?"

"I don't know. I've never heard him mention it before," said Jeff. "Now come on. It's still early. I'll drive you up to the dam myself."

"At this time of night? It's very dark," I said. "And it's about fifteen kilometres."

"And the road has only just been made," said Jeff. "Never mind. Come on."

Chapter Nine

The road up Thunder Creek was like the bed of a stream. Water poured across it. But the big car climbed up and up. There was a moon, and we could see the snowy tops of the mountains. We arrived at the work camp by the dam, and Jeff stopped the car.

By the car's lights we could see the hoist, the wooden platform which raised the materials. It was hanging by thick wires. We looked inside the engine house. There was a huge iron wheel, and the wires of the hoist ran round it. It was connected to a big engine.

"The workmen had the engine running today, didn't they?" I said to Jeff.

"Yes. What's on your mind, Bruce?"

"You manage a garage, don't you, Jeff? Can you start that engine?"

"Yes, but don't be mad, Bruce. You can't go up to the Kingdom alone. Suppose the motor failed?"

We discovered that there was a safety brake. If the engine failed, the hoist could fall slowly down to the ground. There was a telephone line from the engine house to the top.

"I'm going up," I said. "Ring me from the top," said Jeff, and he handed me a torch.

It was a strange journey alone there, as I hung in space in the moonlit night. As I looked down, the valley seemed far away. It was very cold. The journey could only have taken a few minutes, but it seemed an age.

The hoist reached the top and I got out. I looked down and saw the dam below me. The centre part had not been finished at the top, and a stream of water ran down. Then I turned, and I was looking at Campbell's Kingdom. It was a natural plain, high in the mountains.

I went into the small shelter and found the telephone. I turned the handle and spoke to Jeff. He promised to wait for me.

Then I went outside and climbed over a high rock. I could now see the whole Kingdom. My grandfather's home was a little distance away. I could see the low farm buildings, half buried in snow.

I was moving with difficulty through the snow. I couldn't breathe easily in this high place. For a moment I thought I saw a figure standing by the house among the farm buildings.

Then a snow storm began, and I couldn't find my way. I couldn't see the buildings, and I was lost. A glow of light saved me, and I turned towards it. As I got nearer I saw flames rising towards the sky. I took a few more steps and found myself in the centre of a group of buildings. One of them was on fire. The roof fell down with a loud noise, and then the fire died away. Black darkness closed in again.

I went into the main building. By the light of the torch I saw a large room full of shadows. There was a big open fireplace. The place looked as if it had been built a hundred years ago. Most of the furniture was hand made.

I shone my torch and looked round the inside of the building. I could see a kitchen and a bedroom. I found some of my grandfather's clothes there. I took off my wet clothes and put on my grandfather's clothes. Then I lit a fire.

I went over to my grandfather's desk and among his papers I found what I was looking for.

Chapter Ten

There were some maps of the Kingdom with figures on them which I didn't understand. There was also a book which I began to read. It was the story of my grandfather's search for oil, in his own handwriting.

In 1911, he wrote, there was a great movement of snow and ice in the mountains. The rocks began to move and slide, and they covered the gold mines. Many men were killed in the mines.

When the snow melted, my grandfather found that the movement of rock had uncovered a river of oil. But soon afterwards there were more rock movements. When he took a friend to the place two days later, the oil had disappeared under the rock.

As I read, a movement of cold air touched my cheek, and I looked up. The door of the bedroom was open. I turned quickly as something moved in the room behind me. The figure of a man was walking slowly towards the fire. His huge body was white with snow, and he held his hand to the side of his face. It was blackened as if burnt by fire.

It was Max Trevedian. He sank to his hands and knees. He was terrified. He thought I was my grandfather's ghost, returned from the dead.

I felt pity for him, though my fear of his strength was growing.

"It's all right, Max," I said. "I'm not Stuart Campbell. I'm his grandson, Bruce. You know me."

I lit a lamp and spoke to him gently.

"Did your brother Peter send you here?" I asked.

"Yes. He told me Stuart Campbell will not rest till everything is burnt."

I found some food and persuaded him to sit down and eat.

"How did you come up here, Max?" I said.

"On horseback, on the old Indian path."

I was worried about Jeff. He was waiting at the bottom of the hoist. But it was impossible to go out in that snow storm. We both fell asleep by the fire.

In the morning, Max had gone. I went outside and found Boy Bladen's lorries. In one of them I found the figures Boy had written down for Winnick—the true figures. I called Jeff on the telephone by the hoist.

"Thank God you're OK," said Jeff. His voice sounded thin and weak. "Johnnie Carstairs is here. He'll come up with the hoist."

Johnnie had to help me over the side of the hoist at the bottom. I was weak and tired. I found myself looking into the angry black eyes of Peter Trevedian.

"It seems that we've got to lock our machinery up now," he said in a hard voice.

"Leave him alone, Trevedian. Can't you see he's ill?" I could hear Johnnie's voice as if it was in the distance. Johnnie and Jeff helped me back to the hotel.

I slept in my room for hours and it was getting dark when I woke. I felt much better. Johnnie was sitting by the window reading a magazine.

"Feeling better?" he asked. "Boy Bladen has arrived. And he's got someone with him to help us. And that lawyer, Acheson, is coming to see you tomorrow."

My luck seemed to have turned. Boy Bladen brought in to see me an Irish friend of his called

Garry Keogh. He was big and heavy and solid, and he shook my hand warmly. He was an experienced oil driller.

There was some good news for me in a letter from the Bank of Canada. It told me that old Mr. Roger Fergus had given me the mining rights in Campbell's Kingdom. He had done this shortly before he died.

"What do you plan to do, Wetheral? Go on and drill?" Garry asked.

"Yes," I said, "if I can get the money. And I don't mind sharing half the profits with you two."

We agreed then that we three would work together. Boy Bladen took the figures I had found in his lorry in Campbell's Kingdom, and said he would send them to Winnick for a new report. They left me and went down to the bar of the hotel. I stayed in my room, and Jean came in to see me. She looked worried.

Chapter Eleven

Jean's face was white. "Bruce," she said, "your two friends are drinking in the bar, and they're talking. It's all over the town now that you're going to drill a well in the Kingdom. If Henry Fergus decides to go on with the dam, you're going to be in trouble."

"I know that," I said, "And you think I may get hurt."

"Well, a lot of people would be glad if an accident happened to you."

"And you think it might."

"After last night anything could happen. How are you going to get the machinery up to the Kingdom? From now on Trevedian will have a guard on the hoist. And you can't fight a man as big as Henry Fergus."

"I can try."

"You're starting something that will end on a dark mountain somewhere out there. I know this sort of business. In the war I did the same kind of work for two years. I know every trick. I know how to make murder look like an accident. I think you should sell the Kingdom and go home."

"You didn't say that when I first came to see you. You wanted me to fight."

"You were a stranger then," she said. "This has happened to me once before," she continued in a tired voice. "I don't want it to happen again. I'm going away for a time, down to the coast. It's time I had a change. I've been in Come Lucky too long."

"You're running away from me," I said.

"No. I'll leave my address with the Garrets."

She half bent towards me, with a new softness in her eyes. Then she straightened up, turned quickly to the door and was gone.

The next day I went round to the Garrets' house, but she had already left. Both the old ladies were very sad about it. Sarah Garret was crying.

"She ran away. She was afraid of life, like Ruth and me. She didn't want to be hurt any more."

"Do you know anything about her life before she came to Canada?" I asked.

"She was in France during the war, working for the British. She worked a radio for them. She was with her father. Then when he was killed, she worked with another man. I think she fell in love."

"Was he killed, this fellow she was in love with?"

"Yes, I think so. But she won't talk about it."

Ruth Garret came into the room with a box.

"Jean left this for you," she said, handing it to me.

I opened the box when I got back to my room in the hotel. It contained a gun, and bullets. I examined the gun carefully, and saw on it the name Paul Morton.

Paul Morton was the man who had joined my grandfather in his oil company, and he disappeared with the money. Could this be the same Morton? There was no message in the box.

I went down to the bar. Acheson and young Henry Fergus were there waiting to see me. I told Acheson that I now had the mining rights of the Kingdom. I told him I no longer wanted him to have any part in my business.

After Acheson had left, Henry Fergus said, "I shall go on with the completion of the dam. In a

few months from now the Kingdom will be a
lake. I've been given power to do this by the
State. You can accept my offer, or we can go to
law."

"Then we'll go to law," I said.

"You won't get your machinery up there. I'll
make sure of that," he said and left.

Afterwards Mr. Mac came up to me and told
me I could no longer have a room at the hotel. I
was not welcome there. I began to pack my
things.

Chapter Twelve

Two days later I was in Galgary. Boy Bladen and
I heard from Winnick's own lips that the figures
showed there might be oil in the Kingdom. Boy
sent the result to Garry Keogh. Then he left for
Edmonton at once to find the rest of his team.

I returned with Louis Winnick to Come
Lucky. We tried to drive up to the hoist, but
about a kilometre along the road out of Come
Lucky we found a gate across the road. A guard
stood there with a gun. We could not pass unless
we had a note from Peter Trevedian, he said. We
knew there would also be a guard by the hoist.

The only way up was on horseback by the
Indian path. And the only one who could help us
was Max Trevedian.

We went to Max's house, and I managed to

persuade him. He brought us two horses, and rode up with us. I thanked him, and he looked round at the wide plain of the Kingdom and up to the surrounding mountains.

He turned to me. "Do you think there is some place we go to when we die?"

"Of course," I said.

"How can there be a God? There's only this." He waved his hand towards the mountains and the sky.

"Somebody made it, Max."

"Yes, somebody made it. He made animals too. Then somebody else made men. Tell old Campbell I've done what you ask."

He rode away down the path.

"He's a strange fellow," said Winnick.

"Well," I said, "Max hasn't had an easy life."

The sun was setting as we came towards my grandfather's house. Two loud shots told me that Boy Bladen was still measuring the sound waves through the rocks. I was so weak when we got inside that I lay down on my grandfather's bed and fell asleep immediately.

Next morning Boy Bladen told me that he and his two young helpers had had a very successful day. Winnick spoke more carefully. The shape of the rocks proved that oil was possible. But further examinations would be necessary.

"You are one man against a large company," he said.

"How far do you think Henry Fergus will go to

stop me?" I asked.

"Don't rush into this," he said. "At best, your driller may lose his machinery. At worst, somebody may get hurt."

He was only saying what Jean had said. But I wrote to Garry Keogh, telling him the results so far. I asked him to meet me at 2 o'clock in the morning on the following Tuesday at the entrance to Thunder Creek. I said we would bring horses.

I gave the letter to Winnick when he left the next day. I watched his small figure as he rode down the mountain side till he entered the woods. Then I returned down the hill into the plain of the Kingdom.

Boy Bladen was working with his two helpers at the side of the plain nearest to the dam. Boy shouted, "Look, they've started work!"

I turned and looked down at the dam. There was certainly a lot of work going on, and a great many men. They were loading bags of material on to the hoist. And I saw Peter Trevedian watching us through glasses.

At the arranged time Garry Keogh met me. He said he could work for two months, and in two months he could only drill to a depth of fifteen hundred metres.

"We're working with a small crew, little money and against time," he said. "It's a great risk. But I'll join you, as I said I would. But what about my machinery? How am I to get my oil rig up to Campbell's Kingdom?"

"By the hoist," I said.

"But you say Peter Trevedian won't let you use it. How can we do it?"

"I think it can be done," I said, "once."

"It will mean about five hours at the hoist," he said. "How are you going to fix that?"

"I think I know, but I've not worked out all the details yet," I said.

"OK, Bruce," said Garry. "I'll accept your plan and drill you a well."

Chapter Thirteen

In the days that followed, Boy Bladen and his team worked from first light to darkness. All that time large numbers of workmen were busy on the dam. And then there was a great explosion. I knew what it was. They were getting out the rock to fill the dam. The race had begun, and we hadn't even got our rig up.

"How long do you think they'll take?" asked Boy when he got in that night. There was a worried look on his dark face. We went up at night in the moonlight to look down at the work. Huge bright lights showed a big camp round the hoist.

"You won't get those seven lorries up here by that hoist, Bruce," said Boy. "There are nearly a hundred men down there."

"The number of men doesn't make any

difference," I said.

"What about those great lights?"

"We'll need them to see by when we load."

He seized my arm. "What are you planning to do?"

I decided not to tell him. The less anybody knew about it the better. "All in good time," I said. "Let's go back and get some sleep."

But he didn't move. "They're too big, Bruce. And the whole thing is too well organised."

"Then we'll have to disorganise it."

Boy looked at me with his mouth open.

"You're not planning to..." He stopped and passed his hand in a tired way across his face. "No, you wouldn't be so mad. But I wish I could see into your mind."

During the next few days Boy watched me carefully, and he seemed a little afraid of me. Like most Canadians, he thought highly of the law. He finished his work and left for Calgary.

I gave him a letter to send to Garry Keogh. It told Garry to move his lorries to an arranged point not far from Come Lucky not later than 5th June. I also gave Boy a letter to Winnick. This asked Winnick to let us know the latest results.

As he left on horseback he said, "I hope it happens as you want it, Bruce."

"I'm sure it will," I said. "Come straight back."

"Yes, I'll be back in a week."

"Send me a telegram with Winnick's results,"

I told him. "And don't forget to bring me the field telephone. That's very important. And the other things I've asked for".

"OK. I'll remember."

Three days later I took Bill, one of Boy Bladen's two helpers, with me. We rode down the mountain path to Come Lucky. We carried blankets, clothing and food. I also took a bag which contained some of the high explosives that Boy used.

Come Lucky had changed. There was new life in the place, and buildings were being repaired and built. I called at the hotel and spoke to Mr. Mac in his office.

"There's a telegram for you," he said, handing it to me. "And a friend of yours, Jean Lucas, is back in Come Lucky. She was asking for you."

The telegram was from Boy. It told me that the results of his recent searches for oil were very good indeed. He would be back in Come Lucky next Tuesday.

I took Bill with me to see Peter Trevedian in his office. I said, "What would you charge for taking a drilling rig up in your hoist?"

"Get this into your head, Wetheral. Your machinery isn't going up in my hoist," he replied angrily.

"I see," I said. Bill and I moved to the door. "That road up to Thunder Creek was made by the Canadian Government in 1939. It's a public road. Who told you to put a guard on it and hold up private traffic?"

"I'm acting for the Larsen Mining Company."

"Fine," I said, "that means Henry Fergus."

We went back to the hotel and I used Mr. Mac's telephone. I spoke to the biggest newspaper in Galgary. They had already heard part of the story from Louis Winnick and Boy Bladen. I told them the rest.

Chapter Fourteen

Bill and I camped down by Thunder Creek for a few hours. It was quite warm and pleasant. Summer had come to the Rockies. Then we got on our horses and started up the road towards the camp by the dam. When we reached the place where Trevedian had put the gate and the guard, we turned into the woods. When we had passed it, we returned to the road.

I looked up and saw the telephone wires that hung from the wooden posts. The two lines ran between the camp by the hoist, the guard at the gate, and Trevedian's office. I noticed that they could be reached by anyone on a lorry. Then Bill and I rode up among the trees, hiding when a lorry passed along the road on its way to the camp.

A little further up I found what I was looking for. Trevedian's men had been digging holes in the rock. They had then put explosives in, and the explosion broke up the rock. They were using this broken rock to fill the dam. I looked to see if there were any holes left.

I found three. I opened my bag, got out the explosives, and pushed one or two bits into each hole. I joined short wires to them, and covered the holes. Then I marked the places with branches from a tree.

"OK, Bill," I said. "That's the lot." We turned our horses and started back the way we had come. We camped by Thunder Creek for the night. As I lay in my blankets thinking over my plans I wondered if my luck would continue. I was using my army experience, and the success would depend on quick timing and surprise.

The next day, the weather had begun to change. Boy Bladen arrived, bringing a copy of the Calgary newspaper. And he gave me the important news that Garry Keogh was already at the place arranged. We had only to telephone him and he would bring his lorries up.

"Have you brought the telephone testing material?" I asked Boy.

"Yes, they're in my pack." He got them out and gave them to me. "What are you planning to do, Bruce?"

"Get Garry and his lorries up tonight."

We rode along the road till we reached a place where the telephone wires were close to the trees. I told them to stand guard. I climbed a tree and soon I was listening on the wire. I had to listen to Trevedian talking, but he soon finished. Then I asked the telephone girl to give me the place where Garry was waiting.

I told Garry to start moving the lorries and get as far as the entrance to Thunder Creek at eleven thirty that night. Then we went back to our camp and waited.

The weather had changed, and it began to snow. This was what I wanted. I told Bill to ride up the road to the bend just before the gate, and watch the guard.

"At 11.15 the guard will get a phone call," I said. "As a result of that call he should leave immediately. He should go up the road towards the hoist on foot. Open the gate, and make sure he doesn't see you."

Bill rode off. Boy asked,

"Is anybody going to get hurt?"

"Nobody," I said.

"Then why are you carrying a gun?"

I gave him the gun Jean had given me.

"Does that make you happier?" I said. "It's 11 o'clock. Time to move."

Boy and I walked up the road. I climbed a tree close to the telephone wires. I had my phone testing box with me. I fixed the wires on and waited. At 11.15 I cut the telephone wires, lifted my receiver and rang through to the guard at the gate.

"Valley guard here," said a voice. I held the mouthpiece well away from me and shouted back, "Trevedian here," making my voice deeper.

I told the guard there had been some falls of rock three kilometres higher up. I ordered him to go and find out what had happened. He must leave the road and use the quicker way through the woods.

At 11.30 Garry's lorries drove up to meet Boy and me. Garry wanted more information about my plans but I wouldn't give it. I travelled up with him in the first lorry, and we drove by the open gate.

After a couple of kilometres I asked him to stop. I got into the last lorry, and I asked Garry to lead the others on. They would come to a place where they could drive off the road among some trees. I asked Garry to wait for me there. I then followed behind in the last lorry.

I stopped the lorry just past the spot where I'd put the explosives in the ground. I walked back to the place. After a few minutes there was a terrifying noise as the rocks blew out and closed the road.

"What was that?" asked the driver of the lorry when I got back.

"I've closed the road behind us," I replied.

I climbed up to reach the telephone wires again. I spoke to the man in charge of the camp by the hoist. "Trevedian here," I shouted. "Every man must go down to clear the rock."

Our lorry then moved on and we joined Garry, who was waiting, hidden among the trees. We then watched while the lorries from the camp drove past us down the road.

"Now I think we'll risk it," I said. And we left
our hiding place and drove up to the work camp.

Most of the men in the camp had left in the
lorries, but the guard with the gun was still there.
I managed to make him believe that we had
come up with new machinery. This must go up in
the hoist ready for use the next day. One of the
workmen knew how to work the hoist, and he
took us up.

Garry, Boy and I went up in the seventh and
last lorry. As I got out I heard Boy's voice say,
"Well, that's the lot. You're in the Kingdom
now, Garry, rig and all." Then my knees gave
way under me and I lost consciousness.

47

Chapter Fifteen

A week later we started to drill Campbell Number Two oil well. And that morning Jean arrived on horseback.

"Mac says you need a cook," she said. She said she'd come back to Come Lucky after her visit to Vancouver because it felt like home. She brought a copy of the newspaper report of my grandfather's trial in London. I had asked a friend to copy it. I discovered that in an earlier drilling in 1913 my grandfather had to stop drilling at about seventeen hundred metres. They reached some very hard rock, and needed a heavier drill, which meant more money.

At seventeen hundred metres! Would we meet the same trouble? I kept this information to myself. But I watched the speed of drilling.

I felt that Peter Trevedian was just waiting his time. And so did Jean.

And then it happened. On the night of 4th July, Trevedian sent a man up to the rig, and he set fire to our two fuel lorries. He also shot and wounded our guard dog.

The next day I went down to Come Lucky on horseback, and Jean came with me. I wanted to telephone Johnnie Carstairs and ask him to bring up more fuel by pack horse. It would be very slow but it could be done.

At the hotel James McClellan, Mr. Mac's son, met us angrily. He worked for Trevedian.

"If you phone the police," he said, "Trevedian will report what happened..."

"I'm not phoning the police," I said, "I'm phoning for more fuel."

I spoke to Jeff Hart in Jasper, and he promised to talk to Johnnie Carstairs and ring me back that evening.

Jean went to see the Miss Garrets. Pauline, James McClellan's kind wife, gave me something to eat. Jean returned with some bad news.

"I think we must go now, Bruce. There are some men coming up to find you, I think Trevedian has sent them."

Pauline promised to take my telephone call and get a message to me at the Miss Garrets'.

I thanked her and we went out the back way and round to the front to get our horses. There we were surrounded by about twelve rough looking fellows, and I was knocked down. But Jean had got hold of my gun and she fired a warning shot. I noticed that she held the gun as if it were part of her, as though shooting was as natural as walking or riding.

She kept the gun aimed at the men.

"Now get back to Trevedian and tell him next time he tries to shoot my dog I'll kill him."

We got on our horses and rode down the street in silence.

"That gun," I said, "you gave it to me when you went to Vancouver. Why did you do it?"

"I thought you might need it. The name on the gun is Paul Morton. He was my father. He died as a man should die, fighting for something he believed in. He was half French, and he found he loved France more than money, more than life itself."

Paul Morton was the cause of my grandfather's imprisonment. He did not return with the money for the oil company.

"Now you know the truth about my father," said Jean. "Now you know why I had to come back and see your grandfather. Don't let's talk about it again."

We spent the night at the Miss Garrets' house. I was given Sarah Garret's room. I lay awake for hours thinking over my problems. Just as I was falling asleep Sarah Garret came into the room.

By the light of a candle she showed me a box. In it were gold bars, gold dust and precious jewellery.

"Why have you shown me this?" I asked.

Her eyes were wet with tears. "This is all I have left of my father," she said. "He became rich in the Come Lucky gold mine, many years ago. When he died, this was my share."

"Why have you told me this?"

She looked at me for a moment. Then she smiled. "Because I like you," she said. "I had a friend once. He was rather like you, a Scotsman. But he was already married. But I must go now. I want you to know that you don't have to worry about money."

"I couldn't possibly..." I began. But she silenced me.

"Don't be silly. It's no good to me, and I would like to help." Then she smiled gently. "Stuart Campbell was the friend I spoke about. Now perhaps you understand."

Chapter Sixteen

With the help of Johnnie and some friends we took the fuel for the rig up the mountain path on horseback. We were drilling through rock that was quite soft, and we were making good progress.

But as time went on, our fuel was getting low, and the dam was getting nearer and nearer to completion. Then we heard that the dam would be finished on 20th August, and the Larsen Company would begin flooding immediately. They had built a power station near the dam, and they wanted to start working it.

We had been drilling for two months, and the men were getting tired. And then the drill met the hard rock at sixteen hundred and sixty metres. Suddenly progress was very slow. Everyone was unhappy and it seemed impossible now that we'd find oil in time. This is what I had feared when I read in the newspaper report that my grandfather had found hard rock near this depth.

The next day Garry and his team decided to give up the drilling and leave. But then we had a visit from Peter Trevedian, who brought me a telegram from my lawyers.

The telegram told me that Henry Fergus was going to go to law about the mining rights in the Kingdom. They said I had not got the rights honestly.

Trevedian knew what was in the telegram. He thought I would now give up. But Sarah Garret had promised me money. So I decided to fight the case, and stop the flooding.

Trevedian tried to charge Garry an unreasonable amount of money to take his machinery down on the hoist. There was an angry scene. Trevedian left with his three men. And Garry and his team agreed to go on drilling after all.

I went to Come Lucky to see the Garrets. Sarah Garret took me into her room and gave me the boxes of gold. She told me to hide them from her sister, but of course Ruth knew. Sarah put her hand on my arm and led me out. She stopped at the front door of the house, and I tried to thank her.

"Are you going to marry Jean?" she asked.

I replied no, and I told her why. "The doctors have given me only a few months to live," I said. "But that's another secret between us, Sarah." And I left.

I travelled to Calgary to see my lawyer, and put the gold in the bank. My lawyer told me that

Henry Fergus had dropped the case of the mining rights. But I couldn't stop him from flooding the Kingdom. Then Acheson, Henry Fergus's lawyer, came to see me. They were now offering me a big sum of money to give up and leave the Kingdom.

But at that moment I had a telegram from Boy Bladen with wonderful news. They had drilled through the hard rock, and were making good progress. Everyone was hopeful.

I refused Fergus's offer and returned to the Kingdom.

Jean met me. She looked tired but her eyes were bright.

"Have we got a well?" I asked.

She shook her head. "Not yet. The boys are working round the clock. They're down to nineteen hundred metres."

"Let's go down to the rig," I said, "I've got some mail for them and a lot of newspapers."

"They've nearly finished the dam," she said.

"When do they think they'll complete it?"

"In two days' time."

"Two days!" It was a race.

We went over to the rig. Garry and Boy were working and the others were sleeping.

"Winnick thinks we'll find oil around two thousand metres or not at all," said Garry. "And we'll be at two thousand the day after tomorrow."

He was looking anxious and very tired.

53

"If we get to oil," he said, "it's likely to be in the form of gas. That could mean an explosion. I'm worried about my men."

Chapter Seventeen

I helped with the work on the rig, and then went away to sleep. I was woken up with the news that Trevedian had arrived. He wanted to see me. He had a police officer with him. Garry was there too, and he held a paper in his hand.

"Trevedian's just given us this order to leave," he said, handing it to me.

The police officer said, "You've read the notice, Mr Wetheral. From ten o'clock tomorrow morning the Larsen Company can flood this area. They won't have to pay you for the loss of any machinery."

One or two of the drilling crew came in. They looked in silent anger at Trevedian and the policeman. Then Trevedian and the officer left.

We went on drilling. At mid-day the drill was down to one thousand nine hundred and eighty metres. It was very hot. I stood looking across to the dam.

"I don't like it," said Boy Bladen at my side. "The weather is very strange. There's a storm coming."

Then it happened. We were working that night. There was a change in the sound of the engine of the drill. Boy shouted something, and Garry moved quickly. "Get off that platform," he shouted to us. "Run, you fools, run for your lives!" There was a loud noise like a hundred trains.

A figure appeared out of the darkness. A hand held mine tight.

"Well, we found oil," said Garry. I still couldn't believe it. "At least, we've found gas. There'll be oil down there too, I think."

We moved back towards the house. When we were out of reach of the noise of the gas, we noticed that the moon had gone. An inky blackness was moving across the night sky. A strong wind began to blow. Then a wall of water fell on us. It was a rain storm but as solid as if a cloud had dropped on us. Thunder came like a gun and rolled round the mountains.

Somehow we reached the house. We didn't wake the others but took off our wet clothes and fell asleep.

Next morning Jean woke me.

"Quick, Bruce, something's happened." She pulled me to the window. I looked out across a lake of water. There was no sign of the oil rig or the well. The Kingdom was already half flooded. I dropped my head on my arms.

Garry and I took our horses and rode round the shore of the lake to meet Trevedian and a policeman.

"Why have you covered our rig?" shouted

Garry. "You gave us till ten this morning."

"My warning was for the house and buildings," said Trevedian. He looked at his watch. "It's now 9.20. You've got forty minutes to leave the buildings."

"We found oil at about 2.15 this morning," said Garry angrily.

Trevedian laughed. "That's a fine story."

"You know it's true," shouted Garry.

But there was nothing we could do. We were defeated.

We cleared our things from my grandfather's house, and then moved the lorries back to higher ground. By midday the place my grandfather built with his own hands was covered with water to the roof.

I felt weak and ill as I slept in the back of Boy's lorry. In the morning Boy said that we had to have the lorries by the hoist the following day. Trevedian's men would take them down.

That day hope returned to us. My friend Johnnie Carstairs rode up the mountain path with two newspaper men, and they believed we had found oil. They had been with Johnnie the year before, when they found my grandfather's body. Their interest in the story put new heart in me, and I felt I could go on. I made a new decision. I would go to my lawyer and ask him to fight the case.

Chapter Eighteen

The next day, we began to move the lorries towards the hoist. But, to our surprise, there seemed to be nobody there. The silence was strange. We stood and looked down at the dam. The great wall seemed to be leaning towards the lake that now covered the kingdom. We tried to telephone from the top of the hoist, but no one answered.

"Well," said Garry, "the platform is up here. We'd better start loading the first lorry."

At that moment there was a terrifying noise. From the dam, two engineers and some guards came shouting towards us. They climbed up to where we stood. Their faces were white and frightened.

"The dam," they shouted. "There's a break. Water's coming through. The whole dam will go any minute!"

"Have you warned them down below?" we asked.

"No, I can't," said a terrified engineer. "The phone on the hoist was cut in that storm the night before last. I don't know what to do. There are about a hundred men working down there below. They're building the power house. What can I do?"

He tried once more to phone down from the top of the hoist. We looked at the dam, and the lake over the Kingdom. The lake was ten kilometres across. The water behind the dam was increased by the terrible storm the night before last. All that water could thunder down and fall six hundred metres.

"It's that poor material they used on the early dam. You remember, when they first began to build, years ago. It was old and it's begun to break up. The fools!", shouted Johnnie Carstairs.

The engineer came back to us. "Nobody is answering the phone," he said, "and there's nobody to work the engine of the hoist."

I made a decision. My life didn't matter. It was short. Before they could stop me, I went down in the hoist alone. I let it drop slowly, little by little, by hand. I used the safety brake. I had found out how to do this when I first went up to the Kingdom alone. It was terrifying, but I got down.

I went over to the power house where the men were working and shouted, "The dam's breaking. Get back to the camp." Some of the men seemed to be moving away to the higher ground among the woods.

Then Peter Trevedian was there, shouting at them. He told them to get back to work. He thought I was tricking them. Then he saw his brother Max, and shouted to him,

"Max, get hold of Wetheral. I want to talk to him."

Max's huge shape was moving towards me. I said, "Don't be a fool, Max. I'm Bruce, remember? Stay where you are!" My hand touched the gun in my pocket. The men were not moving. They weren't sure if I was telling the truth. If Max got hold of me they would never move in time. It was Max or them, one man or nearly a hundred. I took careful aim and shot him in the right leg.

Peter Trevedian was coming towards me. I raised the gun. "Get back," I said. And I shouted to the men standing around, "Get out of here, all of you. Find high ground. Get your brother out of here, Trevedian."

Peter Trevedian didn't move. "You're mad," he said. He called an engineer, and they ran towards the hoist before I could stop them. Trevedian didn't believe me. He wanted to go up and see the dam for himself.

I managed to pull the heavy wounded Max up the hill towards the woods. I looked back and saw Peter Trevedian and the engineer start the engine of the hoist. I saw it move up.

It was halfway up when the dam broke up. A wall of water rushed down, and the hoist was carried away with it.

I started to run. As the water rushed into the

valley I was half drowned, and thrown against some rocks. But I managed to hold on to Max. I remember lying on the ground in great pain. Max was beside me, unconscious but alive. A little distance away a huge flood of water rushed by.

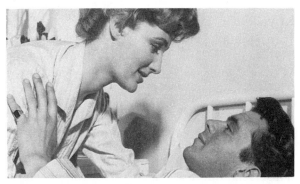

Later I woke to full consciousness in hospital. I had broken some bones, but I'd be all right. At least, that was what Jean told me, as she bent over me. "Don't worry, darling," she said.

The next day she brought me a letter. It was signed by the men who were working at the power house. They thanked me for saving their lives, and promised to help me.

The doctor came in. He gave my broken bones a short examination. Then he gave me a complete medical examination. I told him about the X-ray I'd had in London. "You're wasting your time," I said to the doctor, "I've only a short time to live."

But they X-rayed me again, and afterwards the doctor said, "For a man who was given two to six months to live you've been doing a great amount, haven't you. Don't you think so?"

And he gave me the best news I'd ever had. My disease had left me. "Your general health has been getting better for some time," said the doctor. "There's nothing wrong with you, except these broken bones. I'm almost certain, but I'll let you know later."

Jean, Johnnie and Garry came in to see me. "We've looked in to say goodbye," Johnnie said. "Garry's going to Edmonton to get a new rig. And I'm going up to the Kingdom."

"What're you going up to the Kingdom for?" I asked.

"The men who were working on the power station have promised to clear up Campbell's house. And they are going to build you a house at the entrance to Thunder Valley."

Johnnie and Garry left me, but Jean stayed.

"I won't go till I've told you this. I'm not going to leave you, Bruce. Whether you marry me or not doesn't matter. But you'll just have to have me around."

"The doctor may be wrong about me," I said.

She bent over me and her lips touched mine.

"I seem meant to fall in love with men who are going to die," she said.

But the doctor's good news was true. My illness had disappeared. Perhaps it was the complete change, the air of the mountains. Who knows?

But I can only say that I am living happily now with Jean in the house by Thunder Creek.

A Word Puzzle

Here are 21 questions. Write down the first letter of each answer. Read the 21 letters – they make another question. Can you find the answer to it? Good luck!

1 When Trevedian flooded the Kingdom, Campbell's home was under _____.
2 Who was the son of old Roger Fergus?
3 What animal did Max Trevedian look like?
4 Was Come Lucky a large or small town?
5 Henry Fergus had a plan: was it for oil, gas or electricity?
6 Jeff managed a _____.
7 When Stuart Campbell took a friend to see the oil, it had disappeared under the _____.
8 In what part of Canada is Campbell's Kingdom?
9 Who did Bruce think he would meet in his grandfather's house?
10 Bruce found what he was looking for in his grandfather's _____.
11 Bruce's _____ was Wetheral.

12 When Bruce first went up to the Kingdom, one of the buildings was _____ fire.

13 The storyteller's first _____ was Bruce.

14 Bruce and Max fell asleep by the _____.

15 Garry Keogh was an experienced _____ driller.

16 Jean said to Bruce, "How are you going to get the machinery _____ to the Kingdom?"

17 Bruce first went up to Campbell's Kingdom at _____.

18 Bruce wanted to _____ a well in the Kingdom.

19 Garry asked Bruce, "How am I going to get my _____ rig into Campbell's Kingdom?"

20 The path up to Campbell's Kingdom was known as the _____ Path.

21 Jean said to Bruce, "I've been in Come Luck too _____"